ILLUSTRATIONS AND TEXT BY ROXIE MUNRO

RANCH

BRIGHT SKY PRESS • ALBANY, TEXAS

BRIGHT SKY PRESS
P.O. Box 416, Albany, Texas 76430

10 9 8 7 6 5 4 3 2

Library of Congress Cataloging-in-Publication Data

Munro, Roxie.
Ranch / by Roxie Munro.
p. cm.
ISBN 978-1-931721-37-0/1-931721-37-8 (alk. paper)
1. Ranching—United States—Juvenile literature.
2. Ranch life—United States—Juvenile literature.
[1. Ranching. 2. Ranch life. 3. Picture puzzles.] I. Title.

SF197.5.M86 2004
636.2'01—dc22
2003069616

Design by Drue Wagner and DJ Stout, Pentagram, Austin
Printed in China through Asia Pacific Offset

To

S U Z A N N E   M U N R O   G U B B I N G S,

my sister and the horsewoman of the family

RANGE

In ranching, the range is open land where cattle, sheep and even buffalo graze. It can be an open prairie with small trees, shrubs, yucca, and prickly pear cactus. Sometimes there are vast rolling hills of grass. A range is divided into different pastures, separated by fences.

Find

a rattlesnake
an anthill
3 buffalo
a coyote
a jackrabbit
14 cows
a red-tailed hawk
a snowy egret
a tarantula
a horned toad
barbed-wire fence
a prickly pear cactus

PENS

On the wide open range, cowboys need enclosed areas for doing their work with the cattle they have rounded up. For this purpose, they have built pens, and into these they herd the cattle. Later, the cowboys will guide the cattle onto the loading chute (on the upper left) for transport by cattle truck.

Find

5 cowboys
a windmill
a water tank
a haystack
4 horses
a cattle chute
a lasso
3 sets of chaps
a mockingbird
an armadillo
17 cows

CHUCK WAGON

When cowboys work out on the range, far from headquarters, meals are served around a chuck wagon. Invented in 1866, the chuck wagon features a stout cupboard called the chuck box, and has a hinged lid on the back that can be folded down to make the cook's worktable. Tin plates and cups are used because they're unbreakable and easy to wash. Standard fare is chuck roast, beans, and biscuits, cooked over an open fire pit. Here the cook is preparing sourdough biscuits. Fruit cobbler is a popular dessert.

Find

- 3 horses
- a barrel
- 3 saddles
- a cowboy cook
- a bucket
- a lasso
- 4 cowboys
- a clock
- biscuit dough
- an open fire pit
- a sleeping dog
- a rolling pin
- 5 cowboy hats
- a cook's apron
- a coffeepot
- a dinner bell
- a stack of firewood
- a bean pot hanging on S hooks
- a Dutch oven with hot coals on its lid

CREEK

On the range you'll find a stream or a creek, usually bordered by trees where the animals come to drink. In addition to cattle and sheep, you may see such wildlife as deer, raccoons, skunks, beavers, ducks, owls, and porcupines.

Find

a horned owl
2 wild turkeys
a dragonfly
a striped skunk
a red-headed woodpecker
3 deer
a raccoon
a box turtle
2 ducks
4 ducklings
a beaver dam
a porcupine
a sandpiper
2 beavers
a stone bridge

CORRAL and ROUNDUP

The corral at ranch headquarters serves several purposes, and a ranch will often have more than one corral. In a roundup, cattle are herded together, then divided into groups of cows and calves. Each calf is roped, tagged and given the shots necessary for keeping it in good health.

Find

3 horses
a coyote
2 deer
23 calves
3 gates
a lasso
3 saddles
a cottontail bunny
4 pairs of chaps
a cattle guard
a hay bin
7 cowboys
a cowgirl

BRANDING

In the spring all the young calves are branded. After a calf is lassoed, two cowboys hold it still while a third applies the branding iron. While one iron is used, several other irons are being heated in the fire nearby. Branding is a device for identifying the animal's owner, and every ranch has its own brand, which is a symbol of the ranch's name.

Find

2 horses
a horned toad
3 branding irons
5 quail
a prairie dog
a scissor-tailed flycatcher
2 saddles
3 pairs of chaps
4 cowboys
a cowgirl
a calf
5 cowboy hats
2 pairs of spurs

TRAINING CORRAL

A major aspect of ranching is bringing up horses properly. In the circular training corral, much time is spent making young horses feel comfortable and building up a trust between the horses and the riders. “Gentling” involves stroking the animal softly and talking to it in a soothing voice. In a step-by-step procedure the horse first becomes accustomed to a halter made of soft rope, then a saddle blanket, a saddle, and finally a rider. A “snub horse,” a gentle, mature horse, helps the cowboys train the young horse.

Find

a young horse
2 cowboys
a cowgirl
a cattle guard
a roadrunner
2 saddles
3 pairs of cowboy boots
a hay bin
a coyote
an armadillo
2 gates
a horse blanket
a pickup truck
2 corrals
a snub horse

BARN and TACK ROOM

Horses sometimes stay in the barn, like this mare (the mother) and foal (baby). Next to the barn is the tack room, where equestrian equipment is stored: saddles, bridles, chaps, blankets, and brushes for grooming horses.

Find

a first-aid kit
a mare
a foal
a stool
7 saddles
a cowboy hat
a flyswatter
rain boots
a pitchfork
a pair of chaps
a fire extinguisher
7 bridles
a rain slicker
2 buckets
a barn swallow
an apple
a curry brush
a bird nest with 2 eggs

BARNYARD and ORCHARD

The barnyard is the domain of pigs and piglets. It is also the home of chickens – hens with their chicks – and at least one rooster. While the chickens bustle around pecking for their food, the pigs feed from a trough. Other animals may visit the barnyard, the least welcome of which is the fox. Here he is, sneaking up from the nearby orchard, where a girl is picking red apples.

Find

2 pigs
2 piglets
a rooster
a squirrel
a bushel basket of apples
a pitchfork
a monarch butterfly
a chicken coop
a ladder
10 hens
3 chicks
a horse
a bucket
a pig food trough
a fox
a girl
a wheelbarrow
13 apple trees

SHED

The shed is the ranch garage, where ranchers keep tractors, cattle trucks, horse trailers, and other vehicles. It may also be used as a workshop for repairs to the vehicles and ranch equipment – as well as a perch for the resident owl.

Find

a tractor
a horse
a cattle truck
an anvil
4 hammers
a corral
2 paintbrushes
a barn owl
a horse trailer
a roll of tape
2 saws
a vise
3 pairs of pliers

COOKSHACK and KITCHEN GARDEN

Cowboys rise early, usually before the sun, and head for the cookshack, where they eat a hearty breakfast, and – later on in the day – an even heartier lunch. They work hard, so they need plenty of nourishment. Cowboys love all kinds of food, and like being served freshly-made hot bread in the morning. Favorite desserts are cakes, fruit cobblers, and bread pudding. The kitchen garden outside (fenced to keep out rabbits and other animals) provides the cook with fresh tomatoes, squash, beans, and other vegetables.

Find

a horse
a napkin holder
sunflowers
a bowl of sugar
5 cowboys
tomato plants
a bottle of catsup
a cook
a coffee maker
grapes
salad
9 cowboy hats
hot pepper sauce
a pair of chaps
carrots
a pepper calendar
a pickup truck
a dinnerbell
donuts
cookbooks
fresh eggs
7 pans
a loaf of bread

BUNKHOUSE

Cowboys live together in the bunkhouse. This is where they spend the evening, reading, watching TV, or, perhaps, playing the guitar. After lunch, they often come to the bunkhouse for a short nap or *siesta* before going back to work.

Find

2 pairs of cowboy boots
a guitar
a TV
a sleeping cat
a pair of jeans
a ceiling fan
a rain slicker
a TV remote
2 blankets
a bootjack
a telephone
2 shirts
2 jackets
2 toothbrushes

OFFICE

Running a ranch is serious business and requires an office. The office keeps all the ranch records, not only of the births and deaths of livestock, but of the weight gain and health of each animal, weather and rainfall, repairs and maintenance for buildings, fences, pens and corrals, and trucks and tractors. Along with other financial records, this is where payrolls are settled.

Find

a computer
4 horses
scissors
a mouse
7 cowboy hats
an American flag
a pair of eyeglasses
a pickup truck
2 longhorns
a windmill
a clock
a fax machine
a safe
a calendar

RANCH OVERVIEW

This bird's-eye view shows the range, where large herds of cattle, sheep, or horses are raised, and the headquarters – the heart of the ranch, where the cowboys live, eat, and work when they're not out on the range. Besides corrals, barns, a shed, an office, the cookshack, and garden, the headquarters also has a residence, where the owners usually live. Ranches can be found throughout the western United States, including Oklahoma, Montana, Utah, Nebraska, Oregon, Colorado, Washington, Arkansas, Kansas, Missouri, Wyoming, Idaho, North and South Dakota, Texas, Nevada, California, New Mexico, and Arizona. Texas has one ranch bigger than the state of Rhode Island. Even Alaska and Hawaii have ranches.

Find

- the range
- the pens
- the chuck wagon
- the creek and woods
- the branding corral
- the training corral
- the barn
- the barnyard
- the orchard
- the shed
- the cookshack
- the kitchen garden
- the bunkhouse
- the office

ANSWER KEY

RANGE

1. a rattlesnake
2. an anthill
3. 3 buffalo
4. a coyote
5. a jackrabbit
6. 14 cows
7. a red-tailed hawk
8. a snowy egret
9. a tarantula
10. a horned toad
11. barbed-wire fence
12. a prickly pear cactus

PENS

1. 5 cowboys
2. a windmill
3. a water tank
4. a haystack
5. 4 horses
6. a cattle chute
7. a lasso
8. 3 sets of chaps
9. a mockingbird
10. an armadillo
11. 17 cows

CHUCK WAGON

1. 3 horses
2. a barrel
3. 3 saddles
4. a cowboy cook
5. a bucket
6. a lasso
7. 4 cowboys
8. a clock
9. biscuit dough
10. an open fire pit
11. a sleeping dog
12. a rolling pin
13. 5 cowboy hats
14. a cook's apron
15. a coffeepot
16. a dinner bell
17. a stack of firewood
18. a bean pot hanging on S hooks
19. a Dutch oven with hot coals on its lid

CREEK

1. a horned owl
2. 2 wild turkeys
3. a dragonfly
4. a striped skunk
5. a red-headed woodpecker
6. 3 deer
7. a raccoon
8. a box turtle
9. 2 ducks
10. 4 ducklings
11. a beaver dam
12. a porcupine
13. a sandpiper
14. 2 beavers
15. a stone bridge

ANSWER KEY

CORRAL and ROUNDUP

1. 3 horses
2. a coyote
3. 2 deer
4. 23 calves
5. 3 gates
6. a lasso
7. 3 saddles
8. a cottontail bunny
9. 4 pairs of chaps
10. a cattle guard
11. a hay bin
12. 7 cowboys
13. a cowgirl

BRANDING

1. 2 horses
2. a horned toad
3. 3 branding irons
4. 5 quail
5. a prairie dog
6. a scissor-tailed flycatcher
7. 2 saddles
8. 3 pairs of chaps
9. 4 cowboys
10. a cowgirl
11. a calf
12. 5 cowboy hats
13. 2 pairs of spurs

TRAINING CORRAL

1. young horse
2. 2 cowboys
3. a cowgirl
4. a cattle guard
5. a roadrunner
6. 2 saddles
7. 3 pairs of cowboy boots
8. a hay bin
9. a coyote
10. an armadillo
11. 2 gates
12. a horse blanket
13. a pickup truck
14. 2 corrals
15. snub horse

BARN and TACKROOM

1. a first-aid kit
2. a mare
3. a foal
4. a stool
5. 7 saddles
6. a cowboy hat
7. a flyswatter
8. rain boots
9. a pitchfork
10. a pair of chaps
11. a fire extinguisher
12. 7 bridles
13. a rain slicker
14. 2 buckets
15. a barn swallow
16. an apple
17. a curry brush
18. a bird nest with 2 eggs

ANSWER KEY

BARNYARD and ORCHARD

1. 2 pigs
2. 2 piglets
3. a rooster
4. a squirrel
5. a bushel basket of apples
6. a pitchfork
7. a monarch butterfly
8. a chicken coop
9. a ladder
10. 10 hens
11. 3 chicks
12. a horse
13. a bucket
14. a pig food trough
15. a fox
16. a girl
17. a wheelbarrow
18. 13 apple trees

SHED

1. a tractor
2. a horse
3. a cattle truck
4. an anvil
5. 4 hammers
6. a corral
7. 2 paintbrushes
8. a barn owl
9. a horse trailer
10. a roll of tape
11. 2 saws
12. a vise
13. 2 pairs of pliers

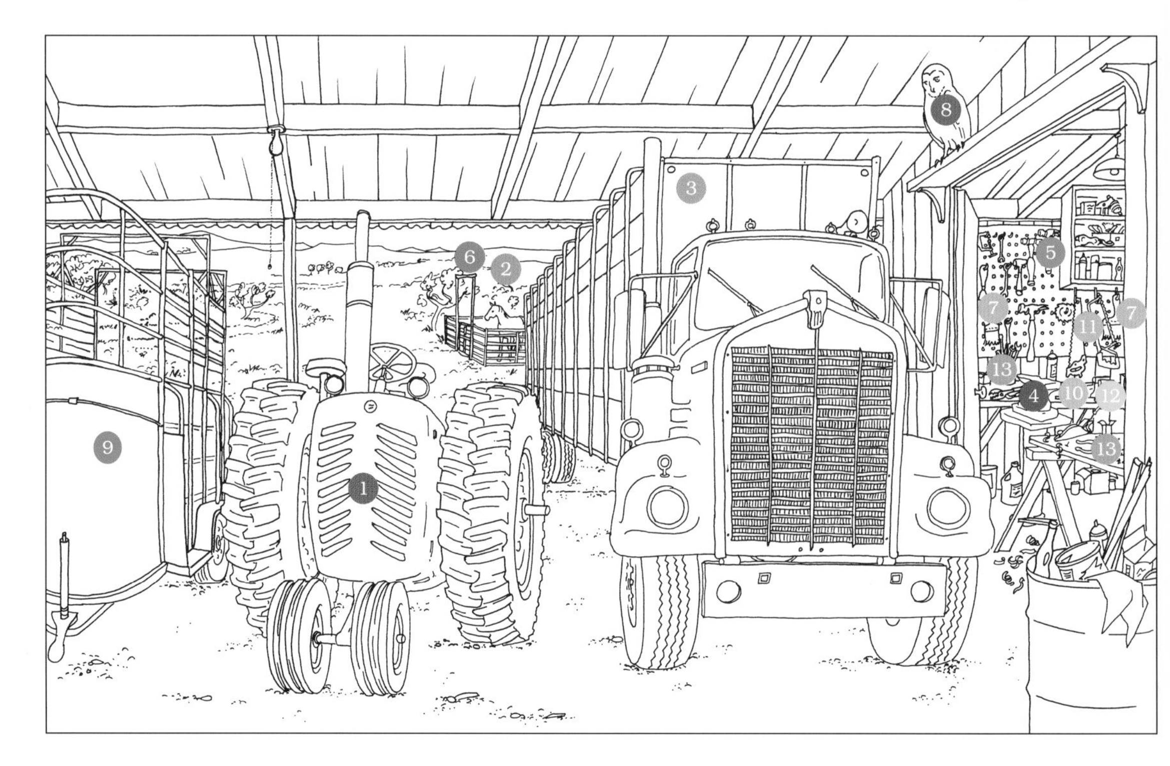

COOKSHACK and KITCHEN GARDEN

1. a horse
2. a napkin holder
3. sunflowers
4. sugar
5. 5 cowboys
6. tomato plants
7. catsup
8. a cook
9. a coffee maker
10. grapes
11. salad
12. 9 cowboy hats
13. hot sauce
14. a pair of chaps
15. carrots
16. a pepper calendar
17. a pickup truck
18. a dinnerbell
19. donuts
20. cookbooks
21. fresh eggs
22. 7 pans
23. a loaf of bread

BUNKHOUSE

1. 2 pairs of cowboy boots
2. a guitar
3. a TV
4. a sleeping cat
5. a pair of jeans
6. a ceiling fan
7. a rain slicker
8. a TV remote
9. 2 blankets
10. a bootjack
11. a telephone
12. 2 shirts
13. 2 jackets
14. 2 toothbrushes

OFFICE

1. a computer
2. 4 horses
3. scissors
4. a mouse
5. 7 cowboy hats
6. an American flag
7. a pair of eyeglasses
8. a pickup truck
9. 2 longhorns
10. a windmill
11. a clock
12. a fax machine
13. a safe
14. a calendar

ANSWER KEY

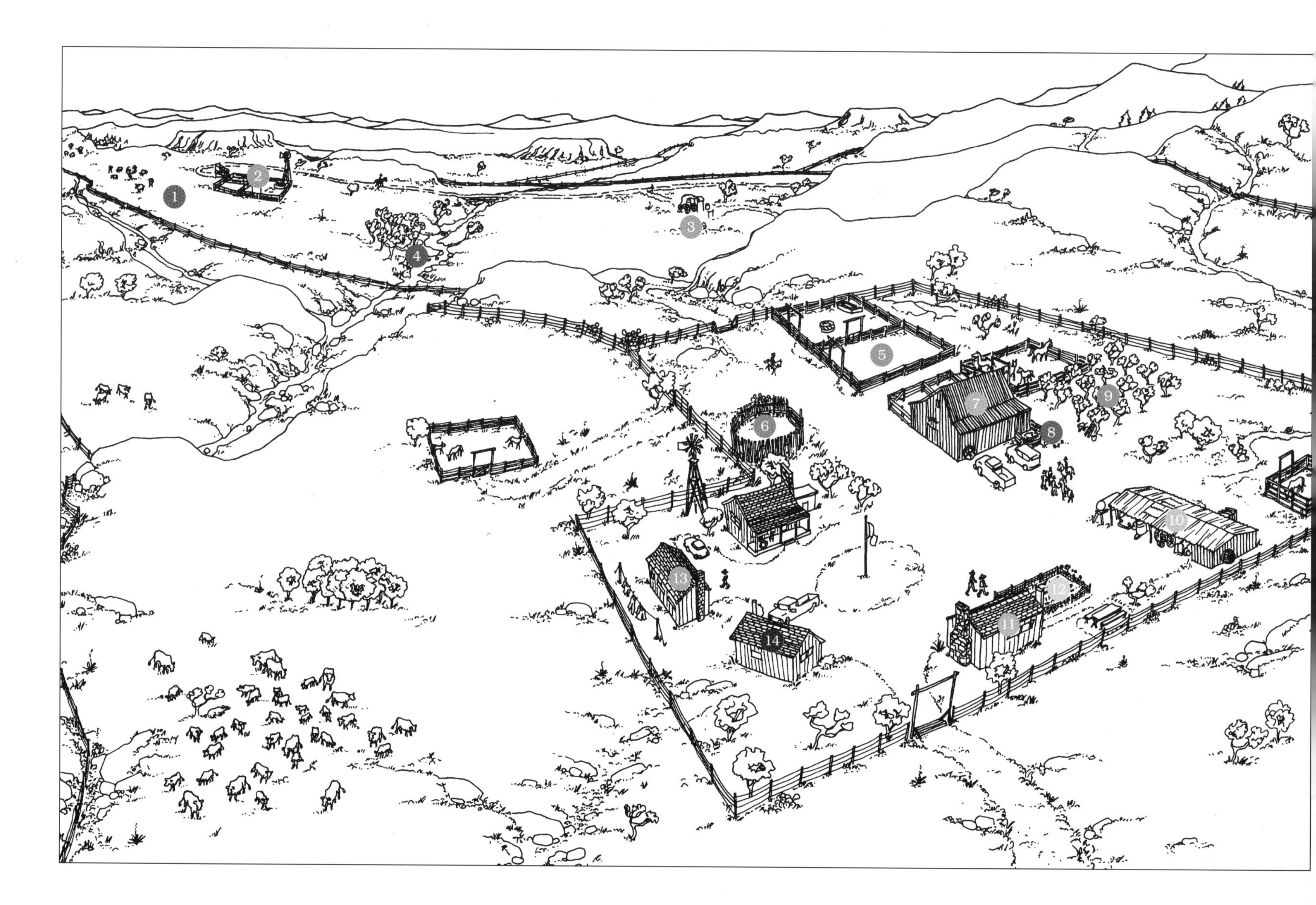

RANCH OVERVIEW

1. the range
2. the pens
3. the chuck wagon
4. the creek and woods
5. the branding corral
6. the training corral
7. the barn
8. the barnyard
9. the orchard
10. the shed
11. the cookshack
12. the kitchen garden
13. the bunkhouse
14. the office